Butterfly Meadow

Twinkle Dives In

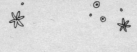

Look out for other BUTTERFLY MEADOW books:

Butterfly Meadow

Twinkle Dives In

Olivia Moss

Illustrated by Sam Chaffey

SCHOLASTIC

With special thanks to Narinder Dhami

First published in the UK in 2008 by Scholastic Children's Books
An imprint of Scholastic Ltd
Euston House, 24 Eversholt Street
London, NW1 1DB, UK
Registered office: Westfield Road, Southam, Warwickshire, CV47 0RA
SCHOLASTIC and associated logos are trademarks and/or registered
trademarks of Scholastic Inc.
Series created by Working Partners Ltd

Text copyright © Working Partners, 2008
Illustration copyright © Sam Chaffey, 2008

The moral right of the author and illustrator of this work
has been asserted by them.

Cover illustration © Sam Chaffey, 2008

ISBN 978 1 407 10655 7

A CIP catalogue record for this book
is available from the British Library

Printed by
CPI Bookmarque, Croydon
Papers used by Scholastic Children's Books are made from
wood grown in sustainable forests.

1 3 5 7 9 10 8 6 4 2

www.scholastic.co.uk/zone

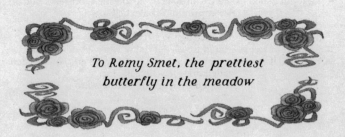

To Remy Smet, the prettiest
butterfly in the meadow

CONTENTS

CHAPTER ONE

Twinkle

It was a perfect summer morning in Butterfly Meadow. The deep-blue sky overhead was filled with sunshine. Hundreds of colourful butterflies perched on wildflowers, slowly batting their wings back and forth. Others wove their way lazily between the tall blades of grass.

Dazzle unfurled her yellow wings and stretched. She'd slept for a long time, tucked away under a large leaf next to her new friend, Skipper.

"Good morning, Dazzle," said a voice above her. "Did you sleep well?"

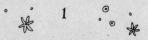

Dazzle slid out from under the leaf and saw Skipper perched nearby, spreading her pale-blue wings in the sunshine.

"Yes, thank you, Skipper," Dazzle called, fluttering over to join her friend. "Wow, it's really hot today!"

"And it's going to get hotter!" said Skipper. She glanced at the sun as it rose higher in the sky. "Let's cool off in the dawn dew before it disappears."

Skipper launched herself off the leaf and Dazzle followed. The wildflowers and the grasses were still covered with cool droplets of dew, sparkling like crystal in the sunlight. The two butterflies skimmed over them, brushing the petals and leaves with their wings.

"Oh, that's lovely!" Dazzle sighed, feeling the dewdrops cooling her down.

"Be careful not to get your wings too wet," Skipper warned her. "Or you won't be able to fly."

The two butterflies rested for a moment on a large, bobbing thistle. Suddenly Dazzle noticed a beautiful butterfly whizzing across the meadow. All the other butterflies turned to stare as she soared high in the sky and turned in a smooth arc. She dived back down, landing gracefully on a yellow daisy. She waved her wings at everyone. She was a much bigger butterfly than either Skipper or Dazzle, and she was a deep-red colour. There were large circles of blue, pale yellow and dark brown on each of her wings.

"Who's *that*?" Dazzle asked, watching as the big butterfly zigzagged across the meadow, showing off her beautiful wings.

"Oh, it's Twinkle!" Skipper exclaimed as the butterfly fluttered closer.

Dazzle watched as Twinkle landed gracefully on a purple foxglove flower nearby.

"Hello, you must be Dazzle!" Twinkle

called out. "I'm Twinkle, and I'm a Peacock butterfly!" Before Dazzle had a chance to reply,

Twinkle began to twirl slowly on top of the flower.

"Look at my wings," she went on. "Have you noticed how they catch the sunlight?"

Skipper glanced at Dazzle. "Twinkle's very proud of her wings, and she likes everyone to know it," she whispered. "It's usually easiest to agree with her!"

"Oh, but I think Twinkle *is* beautiful,"

5

said Dazzle, not bothering to whisper. "I think she's one of the prettiest butterflies I've seen in the meadow."

Twinkle looked pleased. "Thanks, Dazzle, how kind of you to say so!" she said, doing another twirl. "Isn't it hot today? I know the *perfect* place to go on a summer's day like this."

"Where?" Dazzle and Skipper asked together.

"Cowslip Pond!" Twinkle replied.

CHAPTER TWO

To the Pond

"What's Cowslip Pond?" asked Dazzle.

"It's a beautiful place," Twinkle told her. "Especially when the sun's shining. It's not far from here! We can cool off in the water, and the ducks are such fun to be around."

Dazzle narrowed her eyes, confused. "What's a duck?" she asked.

Twinkle zoomed up into the air. "There's only one way for you to find out," she cried, hovering above Dazzle and Skipper. "Follow me to Cowslip Pond!" Twinkle darted off, weaving her way through the clouds of butterflies in the meadow.

Dazzle and Skipper flew after her. A trip to the pond was sure to be an adventure!

"Be careful, you three," called Spot, one of the older butterflies. She was sunning herself on a crimson poppy. "Don't go too far from the meadow."

Dazzle and Skipper didn't even have time to reply. They were too busy trying to keep up with Twinkle, who was zipping along excitedly ahead of them.

"Come on, you two!" Twinkle called. "I can't wait to cool off in Cowslip Pond."

Dazzle and Skipper followed Twinkle across the fields. It seemed like they were flying for a long time. Dazzle was beginning to feel tired when they entered a peaceful little valley. The grass was starred with yellow, pink and cream flowers. A bird sat in a nearby tree, singing with a "tut-tut-tut" sound.

"That's a thrush," Skipper explained to Dazzle. "And this is Cowslip Valley. See those yellow flowers? They're cowslips. And there's Cowslip Pond at the other end of the valley."

Dazzle gazed into the distance and could see the cool, blue shimmer of water.

"Hurry up," Twinkle called. She was hovering in mid-air, waiting for Skipper and Dazzle to catch up. "I can't wait to show you the pond."

As Dazzle and Skipper flew over to join her, Dazzle heard a strange clicking noise below them. "What's that?" she exclaimed, coming to a stop and glancing around in alarm. "Look down there, Dazzle," Twinkle told her. "Next to that patch of yellow primroses. Can you see him?"

"See *who*?" Dazzle asked. She couldn't see *anything*.

A green insect jumped quickly out of the clump of primroses. He landed on a large blade of grass, waving his antennae.

"That's a cricket," Twinkle explained. "He makes that clicking noise you heard by rubbing his wings together."

"Really?" said Dazzle, looking down at the long-legged insect.

The cricket glanced up and noticed the three butterflies hovering above him.

"Good morning, ladies," the cricket called cheerfully.

"Good morning," Dazzle replied.

"Come with me," Twinkle laughed, "I've got something else to show you." She led Dazzle along the valley, closer to the pond. Skipper followed behind them. "See those yellow flowers down there, Dazzle?"

"You mean the cowslips?" asked Dazzle.

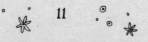

"No, no!" Twinkle replied. "The cowslips are pale yellow. I'm talking about those smaller golden-yellow flowers. They're called buttercups."

"Buttercups," Dazzle repeated, noticing how the golden petals glowed in the bright sunshine.

"Try flying underneath them, Dazzle," Twinkle told her. "Go on!"

Dazzle dipped down and flew carefully between the clumps of buttercups. Suddenly she was bathed in a beautiful golden glow from the shiny petals. Dazzle cried out with delight.

"See?" Twinkle called. "I can show you lots of fun things like that, Dazzle!"

"Oh, Twinkle!" Dazzle said, flying up to meet her two friends again. "Thank you—"

"Ooh, wow," Twinkle interrupted. "I can see a sunflower! I must go and sit on it for a moment. It's so tall. Everyone will be able to see how gorgeous my wings look next to its petals!"

Twinkle fluttered off towards the sunflower, without a backward glance.

Dazzle watched her leave, feeling sad. Didn't Twinkle care what she had to say?

CHAPTER THREE

Pond Pals

Dazzle hung her head. She was grateful to Twinkle for bringing her to Cowslip Pond and showing her all these new things. But she was disappointed that her new friend didn't seem to have any time to stop and listen to her.

"Don't feel upset, Dazzle," Skipper said gently as they flew on towards the pond. "Twinkle can't help herself. She likes to be the centre of attention, and sometimes she forgets that she might hurt people's feelings."

"I only wanted to say thank you,"

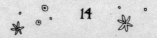

Dazzle sighed, watching Twinkle settle on the large, upturned face of the sunflower. The Peacock butterfly's deep-red wings sparkled and shimmered against the yellow petals.

"Come on," said Skipper cheerfully. "I can't wait to cool off in the water. Twinkle won't sit still for long. I'm sure she'll be right behind us!"

Dazzle cheered up as they drew closer to Cowslip Pond. It was large and round, and it was edged with thick clumps of reeds. The still, green-blue water was dotted with lily pads and it looked cool and inviting. Dazzle couldn't wait to get closer and feel the breeze that was rippling the surface of the water.

"Well, what do you think?" asked Skipper as she and Dazzle hovered above the reeds.

"I think it's amazing—" Dazzle began.

"Quack! Quack!"

"Oh!" Dazzle gasped and looked round to see what was making that loud noise. She saw a little fluffy white bird with a yellow beak standing on the bank of the pond.

"What's *that*, Skipper?"

"That's a duckling, a young duck," Skipper explained. "There are quite a few ducks living here at Cowslip Pond. They're friendly."

As Dazzle and Skipper watched, Twinkle came swooping over towards the pond. "Hello, Feathers!" she called to the duckling. She landed on his beak and gave him a butterfly kiss, fluttering her wings against his brow. "Dazzle, this is my friend Feathers."

"Pleased to meet you, Feathers," Dazzle called shyly as Twinkle danced off again. She could see now that Skipper was right. Twinkle *did* care, really. She just got distracted easily!

"I'm beautiful, aren't I, Feathers?" Twinkle called as she flew over the surface of the pond.

"Quack!" Feathers agreed. Dazzle and Skipper glanced at each other. Dazzle felt laughter tickling inside her. Skipper looked like she wanted to laugh too.

"Watch me air dive, Dazzle!" Twinkle said, dipping down near the water. She skimmed across the surface, her wings so close to the water it took Dazzle's breath away. "Wheee!"

"Be careful, Twinkle," Skipper called.

"It's so cool down here," Twinkle sighed happily. "And I can see my reflection in the water too! Come on!"

Dazzle and Skipper skimmed across

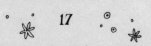

the pond behind Twinkle. Dazzle loved the feel of the cool breeze below her wings, but she didn't dare to get as close to the water as Twinkle did.

"Twinkle's brave, isn't she?" Dazzle asked Skipper as they flew together.

"Maybe," Skipper replied. "But we're much safer up here."

As Dazzle was fanning her wings slowly to and fro in the breeze, she noticed some brown insects on the surface of the pond. They weren't flying like Dazzle, Twinkle and Skipper. Instead they were moving

quickly across the water on their long, thin legs. Dazzle stared at them in amazement.

"Skipper," she gasped, "What are *those*? I've never seen such long hairy legs."

The insects heard Dazzle and looked up at her.

"We're pond skaters," one of them called. "We live on the surface of the pond and we wait for bugs to fall into the water."

"Why?" Dazzle asked.

"To eat them," the pond skater replied matter-of-factly.

"I see," said Dazzle. But she didn't really understand. She turned to Skipper. "Would they really eat another bug?"

"Yes," Skipper replied. "We sip nectar. They eat bugs. We all have to eat."

Dazzle flew higher into the air, away from the surface of the pond. She didn't want to be anybody's lunch.

"Look at me!" Twinkle called. She was fluttering across the water again. "I'm going to do a really low dive this time! Ready or not – here I come!"

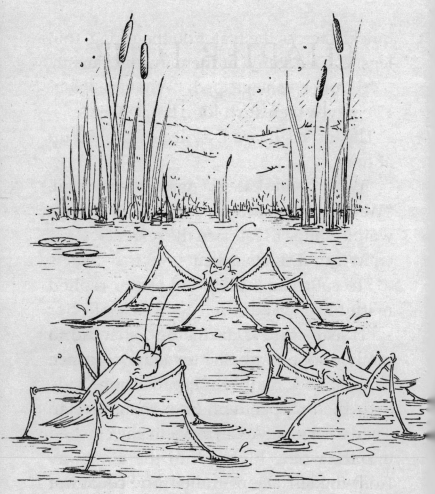

CHAPTER FOUR

Twinkle's in Trouble

"Oh no!" Dazzle gasped as Twinkle skimmed across the pond. Her wings were almost touching the surface. It looked awfully dangerous. "Skipper, she's too close to the water!"

Twinkle tried to do one of her spectacular twirls. But she was flying so low that one of her wings hit the surface of the pond. Twinkle tipped to one side and then the other. She struggled to steady her wings. Crying out, she crashed into the water.

"Twinkle!" Dazzle called. She could see

that her friend's wings were wet now. They drooped and sagged in the water. "Skipper, we have to help her out." "Wait, Dazzle." Skipper rushed after her. "We can't get our wings wet too – that would be a disaster. We'd be no help at all to Twinkle then."

Helplessly Dazzle and Skipper watched as Twinkle managed to grab on to the edge of a fat green lily pad floating nearby. She dragged herself out of the water and lay there, panting from the effort.

Dazzle and Skipper flew over to the lily pad and hovered above their friend.

"Are you all right, Twinkle?" Dazzle asked. "Have you hurt your wings?"

"I don't
think so,"
Twinkle called
back weakly. She
was gasping for
breath. She wouldn't look at
her friends. "But they're soaked
through."

Dazzle glanced down at Twinkle's
wings. They hung limply by her sides,
dripping water.

"So you can't fly up to us?" Skipper
said, looking worried.

"No, I can't fly at all," Twinkle replied, struggling to lift her wings. "I'm too wet. Just look at me. I'm a mess. I'll have to wait until I drv out a bit."

Dazzle and Skipper circled the lily pad, watching as Twinkle spread out her wings in the sunshine. They were still wet and crumpled.

"I wish there was some way we could get Twinkle out of the pond," Dazzle said.

"Maybe
Feathers the
duckling
would help?"
She and
Skipper
looked around
the pond
hopefully.

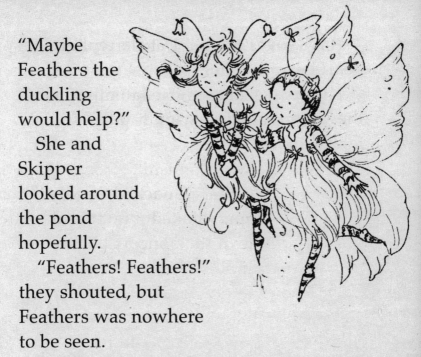

"Feathers! Feathers!"
they shouted, but
Feathers was nowhere
to be seen.

"Well, at least the sun is nice and
hot," Skipper said with a sigh. "That
means Twinkle's wings will dry out
quickly."

Dazzle noticed something moving on
the other side of the pond and glanced
over. She saw the pond skaters staring at
Twinkle.

"But maybe not fast enough," Dazzle
whispered.

Skipper looked puzzled. "What do you
mean?" she asked.

"Look over there," Dazzle replied, her heart beating faster.

The pond skaters were skimming across the water and they were headed straight for Twinkle!

CHAPTER FIVE

Looking for Help

"Help!" Twinkle cried, as soon as she saw the insects skating in her direction.

"Oh, Skipper!" Dazzle gasped, feeling frightened. "What *are* we going to do?"

"We'll have to try and keep them away from Twinkle," Skipper replied in a determined voice. "Come on, Dazzle!"

Bravely Skipper and Dazzle swooped straight towards the pond skaters. Twinkle was trying to move her wings but they were still soaked through. She couldn't lift them, however hard she panted and strained.

"Hold it right there!" Skipper called loudly, hovering just out of the pond skaters' reach. "You shouldn't be coming *this* way."

"Why not?" asked the pond skater at the front of the group.

"Because there's a nice fat insect for you over on the other side of the pond, by that big clump of reeds," Dazzle said. She didn't like telling fibs, but they had to help

Twinkle. "Why don't you go and see?"

The pond skaters turned and skimmed eagerly back across the water.

"What are we going to do, Dazzle?" Skipper asked. "We don't have much time before the pond skaters realize that we tricked them."

Dazzle thought for a moment.

"Maybe we could fly back to the meadow and get some of the older butterflies," she suggested. "Spot or one of the others may be able to help us."

But Twinkle heard what Dazzle was saying, and she looked even more frightened.

"Oh, *please* don't leave me!" Twinkle cried. "I'm scared. I don't want to be trapped here, all alone."

"Don't worry, Twinkle," Dazzle said quickly. "We won't leave you."

"There aren't any insects here," one of the pond skaters shouted from the other side of the pond. "We've been tricked!" He and the others skimmed back across the water, heading straight for Twinkle again.

"We have to call for help," said Skipper. "Someone in the meadow might hear us."

"Good idea," Dazzle agreed. She and Skipper fluttered side by side, hovering just above Twinkle. "OK, one, two three – HELP!"

Skipper and Dazzle called out together as loudly as they could, but their voices were too soft to carry very far.

"We're a long way from the meadow," Skipper pointed out. "I don't think anyone will hear us."

Dazzle gazed around Cowslip Pond,

looking for anyone who might help. But she couldn't see a single butterfly's wing.

Twinkle was still stranded in the middle of the pond and the pond skaters were getting closer and closer. If Dazzle didn't think of something quickly, Twinkle would be in even more trouble. How could she help her new friend?

CHAPTER SIX

Dazzle's Great Idea

The pond skaters were still skimming towards Twinkle. They were only about a metre from the lily pad now.

"Oh no! Dazzle, look!" Skipper said in dismay, turning her face up to the sky. "The sun has disappeared behind that big cloud. That means Twinkle's wings are going to take even longer to dry."

That was it! Dazzle had an idea. If they could do something to help Twinkle get her wings dry she would be able to fly away from the pond skaters. . .

Dazzle remembered how she'd been chased by a blackbird. She had been scared just like Twinkle, but Skipper had come to her rescue. Dazzle had flown close behind Skipper as they darted to safety. Even in all the excitement, the breeze from Skipper's beating wings had been strong.

"I know!" Dazzle said suddenly. "Skipper, we can use our wings to make a breeze and help Twinkle to dry out more quickly."

"Dazzle, that's a great idea!" Skipper gasped excitedly. "Let's go!"

Dazzle and Skipper dipped down to the lily pad. Twinkle was huddled in the centre of the leaf, trying to make herself as small as possible. The pond skaters had spread out and were circling the lily pad. They looked hungry.

"Twinkle, don't panic," Skipper called.

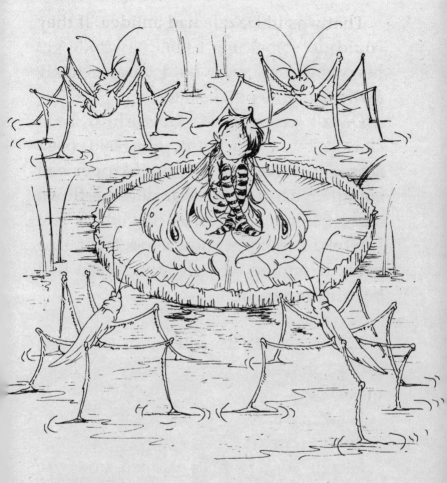

"Just stay still."

"I don't have any choice," Twinkle called back helplessly. "My wings are still too damp to fly!" She raised one wing but it flopped down again.

"Skipper and I are going to dry them

off," Dazzle told her.

Dazzle and Skipper fluttered as close to Twinkle as possible. Dazzle hovered over one wing and Skipper over the other. Then both butterflies began to beat their wings as fast as possible.

"Ooh, I can feel the breeze," Twinkle cried, wriggling with delight. "I can feel myself drying out!"

CHAPTER SEVEN

Twinkle's Escape

"Keep going, Skipper," Dazzle panted. Her wings were aching but she didn't stop fluttering them to and fro. Neither did Skipper.

The pond skaters were still circling the lily pad, their gazes fixed on Twinkle. "What are you doing?" asked one of them, glancing up at Dazzle and Skipper.

"You won't be able to eat this insect," Skipper called. "She's too pretty for lunch!"

"We don't mind what she looks like," the pond skater replied. "We're hungry."

Dazzle glared at him and beat her wings even faster.

"Keep going," called a beautiful, brilliant-blue insect hovering near the lilly pad. "You can do it, I just know you can!"

"That's a dragonfly," Skipper told Dazzle, panting.

"Thank you," Dazzle called to the dragonfly. She could see tiny fishes peeking out of the water at them too.

The whole pond was watching the butterflies now!

There was a splash at the side of the pond. Dazzle glanced over and saw Feathers the duckling swimming towards Twinkle.

"Quack!" he called, flapping his wings at the pond skaters. The insects skated out of his way but they didn't move far from the lily pad.

"Thank you, Feathers," Twinkle cried. Dazzle noticed that she was looking much happier as she moved her wings backwards and forwards.

"I think Twinkle's enjoying all the attention," Skipper whispered to Dazzle.

"I'm going to try and fly," Twinkle announced, giving herself a little shake.

At that moment, the sun broke out from behind the cloud.

"Ah, that's better!" Twinkle sighed as the warm sunshine kissed her wings.

Feathers quacked loudly. Dazzle and Skipper looked down and noticed that some of the pond skaters were beginning to climb on to the lily pad.

"Do you think you can fly now, Twinkle?" Dazzle called.

"I can try," Twinkle said, looking frightened.

Slowly she moved her wings back and forth. Dazzle held her breath as Twinkle fluttered uncertainly upwards and then dipped down again. Were Twinkle's wings dry enough to fly?

Looking determined, Twinkle flapped her wings more strongly. This time she rose up into the air, leaving the lily pad and the pond skaters behind. Dazzle and Skipper clapped their wings in delight and flew after her.

"Hurrah!" cried Twinkle, doing three twirls in a row. "I've dried out completely."

Feathers, the dragonflies and the fishes watched, their faces shining with happiness. Twinkle celebrated by doing a swift lap of the pond, turning her wings this way and that in the sun.

"Oh well,
you win some,
you lose some!"
a pond skater said.

"Let's see
what's for
lunch on
the other side
of the pond."
"Go, Twinkle!" Dazzle
cheered as Twinkle swooped
down to say hello to the minnows.
The little fish were bobbing excitedly up
and down in the water. "We did it,
Skipper!"

CHAPTER EIGHT

Friends for Life

"That's Twinkle for you," Skipper said with a laugh. "Better than ever!"

Dazzle and Skipper joined Twinkle who was hovering by the edge of the pond.

"Thank you," Twinkle cried, swooping towards them and brushing her gorgeous wings against Dazzle's. "It was your brilliant idea that helped me escape, Dazzle. If it hadn't been for you and Skipper, I don't know what I would have done."

"I'm glad you're safe, Twinkle," Dazzle said shyly.

"Me too," Skipper added.

"I'll never forget what you did for me, Dazzle," Twinkle said. "You two know what this means, don't you?"

Dazzle and Skipper both looked puzzled.

"It means that we three butterflies are now friends for ever!" Twinkle announced.

Dazzle was thrilled. Twinkle was a special butterfly and Dazzle had helped her out of a *very* sticky situation. Dazzle felt proud of herself.

"Oh, look down there," Twinkle said, dipping down to the reeds at the edge of the pond. "See the family of ladybirds on that blade of grass?"

Dazzle and Skipper watched as Twinkle flew closer to the ladybirds and hovered near them.

"Hi, ladybirds!" she called. "Look at the amazing markings on my wings! Have you ever seen anything so pretty?"

The ladybird family all stopped to stare at Twinkle. Dazzle and Skipper glanced at each other and laughed.

"Good old Twinkle," said Dazzle.

"She'll never change," Skipper added. "We love her just the way she is!"

"Those are my two best friends, Dazzle and Skipper," Twinkle told the ladybirds. "They saved my life today. *They* are the most beautiful butterflies in all of Butterfly Meadow."

Dazzle couldn't believe it. Twinkle zoomed over to Dazzle and Skipper.

"Do you mean it?" asked Dazzle, as Twinkle landed on a flower beside her. Twinkle nodded as the flower's head bobbed up and down.

"Absolutely," Twinkle said. "It's not all about how you look. It's what you do that counts." Dazzle had never had anyone tell her she was beautiful before.

"It's true," said Skipper as she landed

on a third flower. "You were brilliant today, Dazzle." Feathers the duckling swam past in the pond and gave a loud squawk of agreement. Dazzle was so full of happiness that she couldn't stay on the flower a moment longer. She flew up into the air and drew pretty patterns in the blue sky as she flew over the top of Twinkle and Skipper.

"Come on!" she called out to her friends. The other two butterflies batted their wings and rose up into the air beside her. Together, the three friends flew through the sunshine all the way back to Butterfly Meadow.

Want to know all about the butterflies
in the meadow?

Dazzle

Pale Clouded Yellow butterfly

Likes: Dancing and making friends

Dislikes: Being left out

Twinkle

Peacock butterfly

Likes: Her beautiful wings

Dislikes: Getting wet!

Mallow

Cabbage White butterfly

Likes: Organizing parties and activities

Dislikes: Being bored

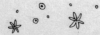

Skipper

Holly Blue butterfly

Likes: Helping others

Dislikes: Birds who try to eat her!

Read about more adventures in
Butterfly Meadow

FLUTTERY, FRIENDLY FUN

Butterfly Meadow

Dazzle's First Day

Olivia Moss

FLUTTERY, FRIENDLY FUN

Butterfly Meadow

Mallow's Top Team

Olivia Moss

FLUTTERY, FRIENDLY FUN

Butterfly
Meadow

Skipper to the Rescue

Olivia Moss

And coming soon

FLUTTERY, FRIENDLY FUN

Butterfly Meadow

Dazzle's Prickly Problem

Olivia Moss

FLUTTERY, FRIENDLY FUN

Butterfly Meadow

Twinkle and the Busy Bee

Olivia Moss

If you enjoyed the Butterfly Meadow series,
then look out for:

The Fairy House

Fairy for a Day

Bluebell
x

Kelly McKain

The Fairy House

Fairies to the Rescue

Daisy
x

Kelly McKain